The Moon In Daytime

For Islay, Roslyn, Chloé, Ailsa, Oona, Aevine and Nono.
Special thanks to Mehdi for all his support.

ISBN: 979-10-97102-00-5

www.lilupicturebooks.com

The Moon In Daytime

By Leigh Kamraoui
Illustrated by Louise Whyte

Late on a warm and starry night,

Alex gazed at the moon shining bright,

And marvelled at the stars that lit up the sky,

Until his eyes became heavy and sleep came by.

The morning sun rose and Alex opened his eyes.

He looked out of his window and, to his surprise,

Saw that the moon had not gone to bed.

It was still in the sky, shining brightly instead!

Why was the moon shining during the day?

Shouldn't it vanish, disappear, go away?

As the bees and butterflies all said goodnight,

The moon in the sky continued to shine bright.

Alex thought, "Now, there's no more day light,

I'll ask some friends who live by the night."

In the moonlit garden, eyes peered all around,

From the trees, under bushes and up from the ground.

The garden came alive with mice, owls and bats,

Hedgehogs, foxes, snakes and wild cats.

In the dark as Alex was becoming much bolder,

A black, long-eared bat landed right on his shoulder.

"Black bat, you gave me such a great fright!

I've a question to ask you, please, if I might."

"Ask away," said the bat, looking very intense.

"Something,' said Alex, "doesn't make sense.

Why does the moon shine during the day?

Shouldn't it vanish, disappear, go away?"

"Didn't you know the moon's made of cream cheese?
In the daytime it sleeps in the fridge, if you please.
"So," said the bat, as its eyes burned golden,
"The moon in daytime means its fridge has been stolen!"

"The moon's not made of cream cheese," Alex stated.

As the bat fluttered off, a bristly creature awaited.

"Hedgehog, I don't mean to interrupt your night,

But I've a question to ask you, please, if I might."

"Ask away, little boy," said the hedgehog, all prickly.

"I'm hoping," said Alex, "to understand very quickly,

Why does the moon shine during the day?

Shouldn't it vanish, disappear, go away?"

"Didn't you know? On the moon there's a swan,

Who lights a book lamp to read 'til it's dawn.

"So," said the hedgehog, as its spines stood strong,

"Seeing the moon in daytime means the lamp is still on."

"A swan on the moon?" Alex doubted. "You're wrong!"

The hedgehog shuffled off and a fox came along.

Alex called, "Fox, you're clever and bright.

"I've a question to ask you, please, if I might."

"Ask away, young man," the fox almost whispered.

"I'm curious," said Alex, as the fox's teeth glistened.

"Why does the moon shine during the day?

Shouldn't it vanish, disappear, go away?"

"Didn't you know that the moon follows me?

Just a few steps behind wherever I may be."

"So," said the fox, as its coat flamed red,

"We've been stalking a hen, and haven't been to bed!"

"The moon doesn't hunt hens," Alex appealed.

As the fox trotted off, two eyes were revealed.

"Owl," said Alex, "can you help with my plight?

I've a question to ask you, please, if I might."

"What's your request?" the owl demanded.

"Can you tell me," said Alex, by now disenchanted.

"Why does the moon shine during the day?

Shouldn't it vanish, disappear, go away?"

"Bat said the moon

is made of cream cheese,

And Hedgehog's moon swan,

I'm sure is a tease.

Fox said with the moon,

it hunted a hen.

Owl, can you help me, my wise feathered friend?"

The owl reflected on Alex's deflation.

With a sigh, it said, "What an imagination.

Wait 'til the sun rises high once again.

You'll get the right answer if you ask the wren."

Hopeful, but tired, Alex climbed into bed,

And dreamt that night of all that was said,

By the bat, fox and hedgehog, each fantasy story,

And the owl's advice from its observatory.

The sun brought the dawn and Alex rose with a thrill,

To find a little wren singing on his window sill.

"Little wren," called Alex, "please, don't get a fright.

I've a question to ask you, please, if I might."

"Ask away, my fine boy," the little wren chanted.

"You'll help me, I know," said Alex, enchanted.

"Why does the moon shine during the day?

Shouldn't it vanish, disappear, go away?"

"Dear Alex, the sun in the sky from its height,

Bounces rays off the moon, all day and all night.

The moon would be dull if not for the sun's rays.

In the dark, you can see it better than in most days."

"Thank you dear Wren," Alex said with delight.

"So, the moon's always visible, but variably bright?"

"That's right," said the wren, pleased to confirm,

Then flew off for a breakfast of a wiggly worm.

Contented and happy, Alex set out with pleasure,

To tell all his friends about his adventure.

Search the sky in daytime and if you're lucky, too,

The moon will shine brightly, especially for you.

Discussion ideas

1. Why do you think the bat, the fox and the hedgehog told tall tales?
2. Which animal had the funniest explanation?
3. Why does the moon appear bright?
4. Why can we sometimes see the moon in daytime?
5. Have you ever seen the moon in daytime?

ABOUT THE AUTHOR

Leigh Kamraoui is the writer of LiLu Picture Books. She has worked for more than 20 years as a writer, editor, and translator of scientific and medical journals.

Leigh's inherent curiosity is continually stimulated by her four inquisitive girls. In her writing, she investigates how the world works by telling fun and educational stories to answer questions that may stump parents.

Born in Scotland, Leigh holds a PhD in Zoology from the University of Aberdeen. She lives in the South of France with her husband and children.

ABOUT THE ILLUSTRATOR

Louise Whyte is the illustrator of LiLu Picture Books. She has worked for more than 20 years as a freelance translator of magazines, editorials, and technical and scientific reviews.

With a passion for illustrating stories in the most effective and entertaining way possible, Louise creates imaginative and whimsical characters based on her love of travel, her children and wonderful nature.

Born in Ireland, Louise studied fine arts and computer science in London. She lives in the South of France with her children.

Printed in Great Britain
by Amazon